Kill Shot

THE JACK REACHER EXPERIMENT BOOK 4

Jude Hardin

June 2017

1

Bees buzzing, flowers blooming, not a cloud in the sky.

It was a fine day for a man to hire an assassin.

Colonel Dorland took his coffee and his cell phone out to the deck. He was working from home today. Or, more precisely, from the personal quarters the United States Army had assigned him to, a one-room cabin on the edge of a cliff, somewhere between Mont Eagle, Tennessee and the middle of nowhere.

Not that he was complaining. His staff—the officers and the enlisted guys—had been crammed into an open bay barracks over at the new headquarters complex, all nine of them sharing a space about the size of a two-car garage. They ate together and showered together and their beds were exactly two feet apart. Less than optimal accommodations, for sure, especially for an elite intelligence unit, but then this was the army. At least they weren't digging latrines behind a row of tents somewhere.

Dorland tapped in the telephone number he'd been given. A woman answered on the second ring.

"Sun River Disposal, Nashville Satellite Office," she said.

"Sorry," Dorland said. "I must have the wrong number."

"Who were you trying to reach, sir?"

"A man named Waverly."

"I'm Mr. Waverly's administrative assistant. My name is Brenna. How may I help you today?"

Sun River Disposal. Administrative assistant. Not what Dorland had been expecting.

"I need to speak with Mr. Waverly," he said.

"Mr. Waverly is in a meeting right now. Would you like to leave a message?"

"I need to speak with him now. Tell him it's Colonel Dorland. United States Army."

"Please hold."

There was a click, followed by silence. Dorland sipped his coffee. Waited. Two minutes. Three. Another click.

"This is Waverly."

"I was told you might be able to help me with a problem," Dorland said.

"What kind of problem?"

"The kind people don't talk about over the phone."

"Could you be a little more specific, sir?"

"No."

"Then I'm afraid—"

"What kind of outfit is Sun River Disposal?" Dorland asked.

"We handle all types of hazardous materials," Mr. Waverly said. "Removal and disposal. We have facilities coast-to-coast. No job too big, no job too small."

Dorland thought about that for a few seconds.

"The problem I'm dealing with is definitely hazardous," he said. "And I would definitely be interested in removal and disposal."

"I see," Mr. Waverly said. "And would this hazard happen to be of an organic nature?"

"Yes."

"I think I understand. I would be happy to meet with you in person to discuss the particulars and provide you with a free estimate."

"Great," Dorland said. "Just tell me where you want to meet. I can be in Nashville in two hours."

Mr. Waverly told Colonel Dorland where he wanted him to be, and when he wanted him to be there, and then he hung up.

2

The sign out front said *USED BOOKS*.

The sign on the door said *OPEN*.

Rock Wahlman walked inside. There was a man with gray hair and gray skin sitting on a stool behind the counter. He was drinking coffee and smoking a cigarette and reading a tattered paperback copy of a book called *Neighbots* by an author named Jesse Lecat. Some kind of science fiction thing, Wahlman guessed.

"Can I help you?" the man said.

"I was wondering if you had any job openings," Wahlman said.

"You want to work *here?*"

There were seven places of business located in the strip mall on Maple Drive. Rock Wahlman had entered five of them already, and he'd spoken to five different managers already. Four of the managers had said no flat-out, and the other one had said to try back in a few weeks. The next place in line had a *FOR LEASE* sign taped to the inside of the window, and then there was the bookstore, which smelled like decades of dust and tobacco and wasted opportunities.

"I could clean the place up for you," Wahlman said. "Straighten the books, put them in alphabetical order or whatever."

"Then what?"

"I'm just looking for something temporary."

"You know anything about books?" the man said.

"What's there to know?"

"You're joking, right? Get out of my store."

"I need money," Wahlman said. "I haven't eaten in three days."

Which was a lie. It had only been two.

The man behind the counter stood and twisted his cigarette into the grungy steel ashtray by the cash register. He opened the register and pulled out a one dollar bill and handed it to Wahlman.

"Here you go," he said. "Now take a hike."

"I'm not looking for a handout," Wahlman said.

"Suit yourself."

The man slid the bill back into the slot he'd taken it from and closed the cash drawer.

"I can unload those for you," Wahlman said, pointing toward a stack of cardboard boxes at the end of the counter. "I can do whatever you want me to do. Heavy stuff, dirty stuff, it doesn't matter."

The door swung open and two men walked in. One of them was wearing a tan jacket, the other a red sweatshirt. They were not big guys, but they weren't small either. Just average. They appeared to be in their mid-to-late twenties, and they appeared to be physically fit. They walked over to a wire rack on the wall opposite the counter and started looking at some magazines.

"Can I help you guys?" the man behind the counter said.

The man wearing the tan jacket turned and looked toward the counter, giving Wahlman the once-over, the way people do sometimes when you're six feet four inches tall and weigh two hundred and thirty pounds.

"Just looking," the man wearing the tan jacket said. He turned back toward the magazine rack, pulled a candy bar out of his pocket, peeled back the wrapper and took a bite.

"You want to make some money?" the man behind the counter whispered to Wahlman. "Get those guys out of here for me. They come in here and mess up my magazines, and they never buy anything. This is the fourth day in a row."

"There's no law against browsing," Wahlman said.

"They make me nervous. They might be planning to rob me or something. Who knows? I'll give you twenty dollars to escort them out of here."

Ordinarily Wahlman would have left it alone, but he needed the cash. He needed it desperately. Some of the money he'd saved from working in Washington and California had gone toward new identities for Kasey and himself, and the rest had gone toward the ragged-out SUV they'd been traveling and sleeping in. Right now Kasey was one block over, doing the same thing Wahlman was doing. Looking for work. Something that paid cash on a daily basis. Something that wouldn't leave any sort of paper trail.

Increasingly difficult to find these days.

Twenty dollars would buy some hamburgers and some gas, and maybe something better would come along tomorrow.

Wahlman walked over to the magazine rack.

"Maybe you didn't see the sign," he said. "No food or beverages inside the store."

"Maybe you didn't see the other sign," Tan Jacket said. "The one that says mind your own business."

"I'm going to have to ask you guys to leave."

"We'll leave when we're ready to leave," Red Sweatshirt said.

"I'm asking nicely," Wahlman said. "For now."

"And I'm saying *kiss my ass* nicely," Red Sweatshirt said. "What are you going to do? Pick us up and throw us out the door?"

"Only if I have to."

Red Sweatshirt slid his hand into his pocket. Maybe he had a knife in there. Or some brass knuckles. Or a pistol. Wahlman was about to reach over and rearrange the bones in his wrist when Tan Jacket tossed the magazine he'd been looking at back into the rack and motioned toward the door.

"Let's get out of here," he said.

"I'm not done looking," Red Sweatshirt said.

"Let's go."

Red Sweatshirt shrugged. He followed Tan Jacket toward the door, turned and looked back at Wahlman before crossing over the threshold.

"Next time," he said.

"Yeah," Wahlman said. "Next time."

Tan Jacket and Red Sweatshirt sauntered across the sidewalk and out to the parking lot. They climbed into a red pickup truck, Tan Jacket on the driver side.

The guy behind the counter opened the cash drawer, pulled out a ten dollar bill and handed it to Wahlman.

"Here you go," he said. "Nice job."

"You said twenty," Wahlman said.

"What?"

"You said you would give me twenty dollars to escort those guys out of your store. I did what you asked me to do. Now pay up."

"I said ten."

"You said twenty."

"I might have some more work for you."

"What kind of work?"

"A guy owes me some money. Two thousand dollars. I'll give you ten percent."

"You some kind of loan shark?" Wahlman asked.

"I sold him a boat. Two grand up front, two more in two weeks. That was the deal. He still hasn't paid me. It's been four months."

"Give me the rest of the money you owe me," Wahlman said. "Then maybe I'll think about it."

"I said ten."

"You said twenty."

The man behind the counter sighed. He opened the cash drawer again, pulled out another ten dollar bill. Handed it to Wahlman.

"There," he said. "Happy now?"

"Relatively," Wahlman said.

The man behind the counter tore off a strip of cash register tape and scribbled something on it with a ballpoint pen.

"This is the name and address of the man who owes me money," he said, handing the strip of paper to Wahlman. "Can you go talk to him today?"

"I never said I would take the job," Wahlman said.

"You said if I paid you twenty—"

"I said I would think about it."

"Well?"

"I'm still thinking."

"You don't want to make two hundred bucks?"

"What if this guy doesn't have any money to give me? Then it's going to be a waste of my time. And gasoline."

"He has money," the man behind the counter said. "He has plenty of money."

Wahlman looked at the strip of paper.

"What part of town is this?" he said.

"It's only a few blocks away. You could walk there if you wanted to. You could be back here in less than an hour."

Wahlman nodded. "All right," he said. "I'll see what I can do."

"You need to leave something here," the man behind the counter said. "Your wallet, or the keys to your car or something."

"Why?"

"So I know you won't run off with my money."

"You think I'm a thief?"

"If the situation were reversed, would you trust me?"

Good point, Wahlman thought. He pulled the keys to the SUV out of his pocket and tossed them on the counter.

"I don't even know your name," Wahlman said.

"Myers," the man behind the counter said. "My name is Myers."

3

Colonel Dorland walked into the downtown barroom and sat in the booth furthest from the door. The room was dark and it smelled like stale beer and cigarette smoke and something Dorland couldn't quite put his finger on. There were about a hundred coats of varnish on the floor. It was almost black. Dorland was wearing civilian clothes. Khaki pants, loafers, flannel shirt with a button-down collar. He looked like a regular guy. He was a little early. Mr. Waverly wasn't there yet. A waitress came and asked him what he wanted to drink.

"Bourbon on the rocks," he said.

The waitress nodded, walked away without saying anything. She was in her mid-thirties and had broken dreams written all over her. Maybe she was a songwriter. Or a singer. Or both. Nashville was full of them. Most of them didn't make it. They came to town with a suitcase and a guitar, and they left with a suitcase and a pawn ticket. Or they stuck around and drove cabs or washed dishes or waited tables. Hoping to be discovered. Hoping for their big break.

Dorland had grown up in the area. He knew all about it. One in a million. Like playing the lottery. A total waste of time and resources, in his opinion.

A man wearing a dark blue suit slid into the seat across from him.

"Colonel Dorland?" the man said.

"Yes."

"We spoke on the phone earlier. My name's Waverly."

"Pleased to meet you," Colonel Dorland said.

The waitress brought a shot glass with whiskey in it, along with some ice cubes and a red plastic cocktail straw in a separate glass. Do-it-yourself bartending, Dorland thought. He guessed it was so you could see you were getting a full shot.

Mr. Waverly ordered a soda water with lime. The waitress nodded again. Walked away without saying anything again.

"Pleased to meet you as well," Mr. Waverly said. "Tell me about this problem you need help with."

Dorland dumped the shot of bourbon over the ice, and then he slid a nine-by-twelve envelope across the table.

"Pictures," he said. "And some background. The man's name is Rock Wahlman. We think he's been traveling with a woman named Kasey Stielson. There are some pictures of her in the envelope as well."

"And you have reason to believe they're in this area?"

"No. But the woman's parents live nearby."

"And?"

"Do I have to spell it out for you?"

"That kind of thing hardly ever works out," Mr. Waverly

said. "More people, more complications."

"My understanding was that you specialize in cases like this," Colonel Dorland said. "If you don't think you can handle it—"

"I can handle it. But it's going to take some money up front."

"How much?"

Mr. Waverly reached over and grabbed a cocktail napkin from the caddy against the wall. He pulled a pen out of his pocket and wrote something on the napkin and folded it in half.

"This much," he said, sliding the folded napkin across the table.

Colonel Dorland reached into his shirt pocket and pulled out his reading glasses. He unfolded the napkin and stared down at the figures Mr. Waverly had written on it—the amount of cash he would need up front, and the amount he would need on delivery.

"That's a lot of money," Colonel Dorland said.

"People don't come to me looking for a bargain. They come to me because I get the job done. Every time."

"This guy is smart," Dorland said, nodding toward the nine-by-twelve envelope. "And resourceful. I've been through two other—"

"I'm not interested in what you've been through," Mr. Waverly said. "I'm only interested in what's happening right now. Today. Apparently it might be necessary to deal with secondary individuals at some point. The risks—*my* risks—increase exponentially when multiple people are involved.

The price is non-negotiable. Take it or leave it."

Dorland lifted the glass of whiskey and knocked it back in a single gulp. He set the glass back down on the table and rattled the ice around with the cocktail straw.

"I'll take it," he said.

"Great. Now tell me a little bit about the primary target. Why exactly is it that you want me to eliminate him for you?"

"I can't talk to you about that," Colonel Dorland said. "It's classified. Top secret."

"I need to know."

"Why?"

"Because I do. I never take a job unless there's some sort of solid reasoning behind the eventual outcome."

"What's your definition of solid reasoning?" Colonel Dorland asked.

"Something other than monetary gain. Or a personal vendetta. Or any number of other selfish or sociopathic reasons potential clients might think are good enough. So tell me, Colonel Dorland. Why do you want me to do this for you? Why this man? Why now?"

The waitress brought the soda water and lime. Colonel Dorland ordered another bourbon on the rocks, and then he took a deep breath and told Mr. Waverly everything.

4

Wahlman walked over to Oak Street, saw Kasey coming out of a seafood place called Portly Joe's Seafood Place. There were two park benches near the front entrance, out on the sidewalk beside some newspaper machines. Kasey sat on one of the benches. She looked exhausted. And sad. Wahlman walked over there and sat down beside her.

"Not hiring," she said.

"Let's go inside and eat," Wahlman said.

"You have money?"

"I have twenty dollars. I'll have more in a little while."

"How did you get twenty dollars?"

"I kicked some guys out of a bookstore over on Maple."

"The owner actually hired you to do that?"

"He did. Now he wants me to go collect on a boat he sold four months ago."

"I thought we said nothing illegal," Kasey said.

"How is that illegal?"

"You're supposed to beat the guy up if he doesn't pay you, right? I'm pretty sure that's against the law."

"I'm not going to beat the guy up. Unless he tries to start something. Last time I checked, it was still perfectly legal to defend yourself."

"You can't go around intimidating people. He could call the police and—"

"Okay," Wahlman said. "I won't do it."

"How much money are we talking about?"

"Two hundred dollars."

"Do it. But I'm coming with you."

"Want to get something to eat first?"

"No. Let's do the job first."

"I had to leave the car keys for collateral," Wahlman said. "It's a long walk."

"You gave someone our car keys? What if—"

"Don't worry. I'll get the keys back."

"And what if you don't?"

"You have the other set, right?"

"They're in the glove compartment."

A red pickup truck pulled into the parking lot in front of the seafood place. Wahlman could see the driver and the passenger through the windshield. Tan Jacket and Red Sweatshirt. They climbed out of the truck and started walking toward the benches. Tan Jacket was carrying a hammer.

"Still have the gun in your purse?" Wahlman said.

"Also in the glove compartment. Why?"

"Go inside and get us a table. We're going to eat first."

"Why is that man carrying a hammer?" Kasey said.

"Maybe he's going to fix that loose piece of trim on the window over there."

"Are those the guys you kicked out of the bookstore?"

"Yes."

"They followed you here?"

"Apparently. Go inside and get us a table."

Kasey didn't move.

Tan Jacket and Red Sweatshirt stepped up onto the sidewalk.

"This your wife?" Tan Jacket said, nodding toward Kasey.

"You guys should turn around and walk back to your truck," Wahlman said.

"Why should we do that?" Tan Jacket said.

"To save money on your next dry cleaning bill," Wahlman said. "Bloodstains are a bitch."

Red Sweatshirt laughed.

"Maybe we just stopped here to try the shrimp platter," he said.

"Not your scene," Wahlman said. "They have napkins and silverware and stuff."

Tan Jacket took a step forward. Lips snarling, neck muscles bulging, fingers wrapped tightly around the handle of the hammer. Wahlman figured he was fixing to rear back and take a swing, and he figured the best defense against such a maneuver was to stop it before it happened. Using the back of the bench for leverage, he buried the heel of his right boot in Tan Jacket's solar plexus, driving his diaphragm up toward his throat, knocking the air out of his lungs and dropping him on the sidewalk in a gasping, quivering heap.

Red Sweatshirt slid his hand into the same pocket he'd slid it into at the bookstore, but before he had a chance to pull out whatever kind of weapon he had in there, a young man and a young woman walked out of the restaurant together.

Early twenties. Maybe still in college. Polo shirts and khaki pants and deck shoes that had probably never been anywhere near a deck.

"What happened to him?" the young man said, gesturing toward Tan Jacket, who was still doubled over on the sidewalk.

"I did that thing you're supposed to do when someone's choking," Wahlman said. "But I think I did it wrong."

"He was choking?"

"He might have been. I didn't want to take any chances."

"Want me to call an ambulance?" the young man said.

Wahlman glanced over at Red Sweatshirt.

"How about it?" Wahlman said. "Want him to call an ambulance? You're going to need one for sure if you don't get that hand out of your pocket."

Red Sweatshirt took his hand out of his pocket.

"We'll be okay," he said, helping Tan Jacket to a standing position and guiding him back toward the red pickup truck.

The young man looked at Wahlman and shrugged.

Wahlman shrugged back at him.

The young man pushed some coins into one of the newspaper machines, opened the door and pulled out a newspaper, and then he and the young woman walked to their car in the parking lot.

Wahlman reached over and picked up the hammer. He walked over to the window and tapped the loose piece of trim back into place. It had been bugging him since he got there.

"Let's go make some money," he said.

5

Johnny Cappulista lived on a quiet street in a quiet subdivision. There was a newspaper on the porch and mail in the mailbox and no car in the driveway. Wahlman walked to the side of the house and peeked over the wooden privacy fence. The boat was in the backyard. It was an aluminum fishing boat. No motor, and one of the tires on the trailer was flat.

"I want to see," Kasey said.

"Okay."

Wahlman laced his hands together, creating a stirrup. Kasey stepped into it and lifted herself up to the top of the fence.

"He paid four thousand dollars for that?" she said.

"Maybe it was in better shape when he bought it," Wahlman said. "And there's probably a motor somewhere. Maybe it's a nice one."

Kasey climbed down.

"Think anyone's home?" she said.

"Doesn't look like it."

"Might as well check and see."

Wahlman nodded.

They walked back around to the front of the house and mounted the porch.

Wahlman knocked on the door.

A woman wearing a white terrycloth bathrobe answered. Her eyes were bloodshot and her skin was pale. She'd been drinking. Wahlman could smell it. Rum, he thought, along with some kind of citrus juice. Grapefruit, maybe. She was holding a cordless hairdryer, an expensive solar-powered model Wahlman had seen advertised on television.

"Mrs. Cappulista?" he said.

"Yes."

"I was wondering if I might have a word with your husband."

"He's at work. Is there something I can help you with?"

"It's about the boat," Wahlman said.

"What about it?"

"Are you familiar with Mr. Myers, over at the bookstore on Maple?"

"Never heard of him."

"He sold the boat to your husband four months ago. Your husband paid half up front. I was commissioned to collect the balance due."

"And how much is the balance due?" Mrs. Cappulista said.

"Two thousand," Wahlman said.

Mrs. Cappulista laughed. "He paid four thousand dollars for that piece of shit? You can go ahead and tow it away for all I care. The motor's in the garage."

"Mr. Myers isn't interested in—"

"You're going to have to talk to Johnny," Mrs. Cappulista said.

She slammed the door shut.

"Nice," Kasey said. "Now what?"

"Now we sit here and wait for Johnny to come home," Wahlman said.

"I'm hungry."

"Me too."

"Let's go get something to eat. Then we can come back and wait."

"Okay."

They walked back out to the main road and crossed over to a cluster of chain restaurants and fast food joints.

"Over there," Kasey said. "Beef ribs every Tuesday. All you can eat. Today's Tuesday, right?"

"It is," Wahlman said.

"What do you think?"

"Sounds good to me."

They walked into the budget steakhouse and followed the hostess to a booth near the back of the dining area. Wahlman sat on the side facing the door. Always on the lookout. Always acutely aware of his surroundings. The hostess brought menus and glasses of ice water, and a few minutes later a waitress came and asked if they were ready to order.

"We both want the special," Wahlman said.

"Comes with two sides," the waitress said. "Most people get the baked potato and the coleslaw."

Wahlman looked across the table at Kasey. She nodded. "That's fine," Wahlman said.

"Great. I'll have that out for you in just a few minutes." The waitress walked away.

"There's a public library across the street," Kasey said. "Did you see it?"

"I did."

"Maybe we can stop there after we finish with Johnny Cappulista."

"I don't see the point," Wahlman said.

"We can't just give up. We can't keep living like this forever."

It already felt like forever, Wahlman thought. He'd been on the run for seven months. A New Orleans homicide detective named Collins was trying to track him down and have him arrested, and an army colonel named Dorland was trying to track him down and have him killed. At least the army colonel was supposedly named Dorland. Wahlman still hadn't found any evidence that an officer going by that name actually existed.

It had all started in New Orleans. Last year, in October.

Wahlman had discovered some remarkable things about himself since then. He'd discovered that he was a clone, an exact genetic duplicate of a former army officer named Jack Reacher. He'd discovered that he and a man named Darrel Renfro had been created in a laboratory from cells extracted over a hundred years ago, and that somewhere along the line someone had decided to erase every speck of evidence that the experiment had ever taken place, including the two

23

human beings who had resulted from the experiment. Renfro was dead now—stabbed inside the diesel rig he'd been driving—and Wahlman was next on the list. His entire existence had been a lie, and now his entire existence depended on finding out why all this was happening and exposing the people responsible.

Kasey had been traveling with him for the past few weeks. He loved her, and he enjoyed having her with him, but he wasn't sure how much more she could take. She had a teenage daughter to think about, for one thing.

Natalie.

She was currently staying with Kasey's parents, at their lake house, which was probably the safest place for her to be, but Wahlman could tell that Kasey missed her fiercely, every moment of every day.

Which was totally understandable, of course, and totally exacerbated by the fact that any sort of contact could potentially put everyone involved in great danger.

"I don't think the library is going to be of much help to us anymore," Wahlman said. "We've researched every military database that's available to the public. There aren't any officers currently on active duty with the last name of Dorland."

"It's probably a codename. Like you said before."

"Right."

"Or maybe Mr. Tyler was lying."

"Right again."

"I know all that," Kasey said. "But maybe if we keep looking—"

"We're not going to find anything on the internet," Wahlman said. "We're going to have to break into the army's restricted databases, somehow. We're going to have to find someone on the inside willing to help us get to the bottom of all this."

"And how do you suggest we do that?"

"I'm not sure yet."

The waitress brought the food. Ribs, potatoes, coleslaw. The ribs were huge prehistoric-looking things. Wahlman picked one up and took a bite. The meat was tender and flavorful. Just the right amount of smoke, just the right amount of sauce. He stripped the bone clean in about thirty seconds.

"Good?" Kasey asked.

"Good," Wahlman said.

"I guess you can't really worry about table manners with something like this."

"No. You just have to dig right in."

Kasey dug right in.

There wasn't a lot of conversation over the next twenty minutes or so. They sat there slurping and gnawing, feasting like a couple of ravenous cave dwellers, chewing and swallowing in a continuous rhythmic gluttonous glow, looking up and smiling at each other occasionally, bonded by the hunger, the experience more than just the sharing of a meal, more like some kind of blissful existential fusion. They finished the first order of ribs, and then asked for seconds. And thirds. And fourths. By the time they finished, there was a pile of bones about a foot high on the center of the table.

The waitress came by and filled their water glasses.

"Anyone ready for dessert?" she said.

Kasey laughed. "Not unless you want to push me out of here in a wheelbarrow," she said.

Wahlman paid and they exited the restaurant and headed back toward Johnny Cappulista's house. When they got there, Wahlman noticed right away that the mailbox was empty. Someone had gotten the mail out of the box, but there was still no car in the driveway.

"Want to sit on the porch and wait?" Wahlman said.

"I'm not sure that's such a good idea," Kasey said.

Wahlman glanced toward the door. Mrs. Cappulista was standing there. She was still in her bathrobe, but there was no fancy hairdryer in her hand this time.

This time, she was holding a double-barrel shotgun.

6

Wahlman took a step toward the porch, positioning himself between where Mrs. Cappulista was standing and where Kasey was standing. He didn't think that Mrs. Cappulista would have walked out to the mailbox in her bathrobe. He figured Johnny was in the house now. Or maybe he'd been there all along. Maybe his car was in the garage, along with the boat motor.

"I need to talk to Johnny," Wahlman said.

"Go away," Mrs. Cappulista said.

Wahlman wondered if she'd finished the bottle of rum she'd been working on. Her eyes had moved a notch closer to the batshit zone on the crazy meter since last time she answered the door.

"Give me two thousand in cash," Wahlman said. "Then I'll go away."

"I could shoot you."

"But you won't."

"Johnny's at work."

"I don't think so," Wahlman said. "I think he's there in

the house with you."

"You need to leave us alone," Mrs. Cappulista said.

She and the shotgun disappeared into the shadows, and then the door slammed shut again.

"Maybe he just doesn't have any money to give you," Kasey said.

"Myers said he has plenty."

"Maybe Myers was lying."

"Why would he have done that?" Wahlman said. "Why would he have sent me over here on a wild goose chase?"

"I don't know."

Wahlman stood there and stared at the house for a few seconds, considering their options.

"Mrs. Cappulista said we could take the boat and the motor if we want to," he said.

"But we don't want to."

"But we might have to."

"What are we going to do with a boat?" Kasey said.

"Sell it," Wahlman said. "We could probably get three grand for it, assuming the motor is okay. We could take Myers his two, and keep one for ourselves. Plus the commission."

"The trailer has a flat tire."

"There's a can of Fix-A-Flat in the car."

"Which we don't have the keys to," Kasey said.

"I was a master-at-arms in the navy," Wahlman said. "I dealt with criminals on a daily basis."

"So?"

"So there are ways to get into a car without the keys."

They walked back up to the main road, headed toward the discount superstore where they'd parked the SUV.

"Who are we going to sell it to?" Kasey asked.

"Huh?"

"The boat. We need to sell it quick, right? As in *immediately*. Today. Right now. How are we going to do that?"

"Myers didn't give me any sort of time limit. We don't necessarily have to sell it today."

"But we need money today. We're broke."

"True."

"So who are we going to sell it to?"

"I don't know," Wahlman said. "Want to just forget about it?"

Kasey stopped in her tracks.

"I'm tired of this shit," she said. "Sleeping in the car. Not knowing where our next meal is coming from. It's been almost two months, and we're not any closer to finding the people responsible for all this than when we started."

"I don't know what to tell you," Wahlman said.

"That's your answer? You don't know what to tell me?"

"Let's just get the car. Then we'll get the boat, and then we'll figure out what to do next."

Tears welled in Kasey's eyes. Wahlman put his arm around her, pulled her in close. She started sobbing against his chest.

"I need to see my daughter," she said.

"I know you do. We'll figure out a way for that to happen after we sell the boat."

"Promise?"

"Promise."

Kasey wiped the tears from her eyes. They walked on. Past Oak Street, where Kasey had checked for work at the seafood place. Past Maple Drive, where Wahlman had checked for work at the bookstore. They crossed the thoroughfare at the next intersection, walked across the grassy area that bordered the superstore's parking lot.

"Didn't we park right over there?" Kasey said.

"We did," Wahlman said.

The SUV was gone.

7

The sign out front said *USED BOOKS.*

The sign on the door said *CLOSED.*

"It's only four o'clock," Kasey said. "Who closes a bookstore at four o'clock?"

"Maybe he stepped out for something to eat," Wahlman said.

"He stole our car."

"We don't know that for sure."

"The car's gone. He's gone. What other explanation—"

"He didn't even know where it was parked," Wahlman said.

"He knew it was around here somewhere. He could have walked around pressing the button on the fob until he found it."

"I guess that's possible."

"Everything we own is in that car," Kasey said. "We have to get it back."

"We will."

Kasey had a cell phone in her purse, a cheap throwaway

she'd bought out in California. She pulled it out and flipped it open and punched in a number. Wahlman stood there and listened to her end of the conversation. She was talking to her dad. She was telling him she'd decided to come and visit for a few days. Yes, she needed money. Yes, there was a money transfer service nearby. Right down at the other end of the sidewalk she was standing on.

"I'll call you back in a little while," she said. "I love you too, Dad."

She clicked off and dropped the phone back into her purse.

"You're leaving me?" Wahlman said.

"I have to see Natalie. She's out on a houseboat with some of my parents' friends right now, but she'll be back day after tomorrow. You can come with me if you want to. Dad's going to drive up to the house in Nashville to get an air mattress for me to sleep on. It's a queen, so—"

"I thought you told your parents to stay away from that house."

"It'll just be for a few minutes."

"We still need to find the car," Wahlman said.

"Dad said he would pay for plane tickets."

"We can't fly. You know that."

"I guess I wasn't thinking," Kasey said. "Bus tickets then."

"I thought you didn't want me to—"

"The army doesn't know about the lake house. I think it'll be all right."

Wahlman didn't like the idea. He had a target on his

back. Maybe he could spend some time with Kasey's family when this was all over. But not now. It just wasn't safe.

"You go," he said. "Take a cab to the bus station. I'll stay and deal with the situation here."

"Are you sure?"

"I'm sure."

They walked to the pharmacy at the end of the strip mall. There was a sign advertising the money transfer service in the window, behind the security bars. Wahlman had been in there earlier, asking about temporary employment. The manager hadn't been very polite about telling him no. Maybe she'd thought he was casing the place. Pharmacies had become prime targets for thieves in recent years.

"Aren't you coming in?" Kasey said.

"I'll wait out here."

"Okay. I'll be back in a few minutes."

Wahlman sat on the curb and waited. Traffic was starting to get heavy out on the main road. People coming home from work. Stopping for groceries or beer or whatever. Just everyday people doing everyday things. Surviving the day-to-day grind. Working and talking, eating and drinking, laughing and crying. Doing the same things people did in every town, large and small, all across the country, all around the world. They had mortgages and car payments and kids who needed braces. Their bosses were assholes and their parents were getting old and the dogs next door barked in the middle of the night sometimes.

Wahlman wondered how many of them took a little time every day to think about how good they had it.

Kasey exited the pharmacy. She sat on the curb next to Wahlman and handed him an envelope.

"What's this?" he said.

"I want you to get a room. And something to eat. That should be enough for a few days."

"Tell your dad I'll pay him back."

Kasey nodded. She called a cab, and then she gave Wahlman the cell phone. She told him she would get another one when she got to Tennessee.

"Try not to accidentally drop it in the toilet, like you did that one time," she said.

"Who said it was an accident?" Wahlman said.

Kasey laughed. She knew how much Wahlman disliked cell phones.

"If something does happen, use Message Moi," she said. "You still remember the password, right?"

"Of course."

Message Moi was a free voicemail service you could access through the company's website or through any touchtone phone. It came in handy for people who didn't want to own a cell phone and for people who didn't want to give out their phone numbers for one reason or another.

Wahlman didn't want Kasey to leave, but he knew that she had to. The car came and she kissed him and told him that she loved him and left him standing there alone on the sidewalk.

8

Wahlman waited outside the bookstore until it was almost dark. Myers never came. Kasey was probably right. He probably walked around with the fob until he found the car, and then he probably took it. Maybe he'd thought that Wahlman was taking too long on the little assignment he'd sent him on. Maybe he'd given up on ever getting his two thousand dollars.

Wahlman wasn't sure what he should do now. He couldn't call the police and report the car stolen. They might scan his ID and run it through the National Facial Recognition Database and discover the warrant for his arrest down in Louisiana. And the name on the vehicle registration and the name on his current driver's license didn't even match. Calling the police was out of the question. He could walk back down to Johnny Cappulista's house and try to be a little more persuasive with his collection efforts, but his gut instincts and Johnny's rum-swilling shotgun-toting wife were telling him that any further discourse along those lines would be counterproductive, at least for the immediate future. He supposed the best course of action would be to forget about the boat for now and come back to the bookstore in the morning. Then he could explain the situation to Myers and try to work something out.

He walked out to the main road and took a left. There were some hotels down by the interstate. A two mile walk, but it was a nice evening. Clear skies, low sixties.

Wahlman didn't have anything with him except the clothes on his back and his wallet and the phone Kasey had given him. He didn't even have a toothbrush. He thought about stopping to buy one, but then he remembered that most hotels will give you those kinds of things for free. No point in spending money when you don't have to. His belly was still full from the ribs, so food wouldn't be an issue until tomorrow. Maybe a snack later tonight from a vending machine. Maybe a candy bar or something.

The cell phone trilled. Wahlman pulled it out of his pocket and looked at it. The caller ID said *BLOCKED*. Probably Kasey's dad, Wahlman thought. Or her mom. They probably weren't aware that Kasey didn't have the phone anymore.

Wahlman flipped the phone open and answered the call.

"Mr. Wahlman?" a male voice said.

"Who's this?"

"I'm trying to reach a Mr. Rock Wahlman."

"May I ask who's calling?"

"Are you Rock Wahlman?"

"That depends. What do you want?"

"It's a simple yes or no question," the caller said. "Are you Rock Wahlman?"

Wahlman wasn't sure how to respond. Kasey wouldn't have told anyone his real name. Not even her parents. Which meant that the caller had gotten his name from someone else. But then how had the caller gotten the number to this phone? As far as Wahlman knew, Kasey hadn't given the number to anyone except her parents. Her mother, and her father. Which meant that one of them must have given the number to the caller. Which meant that the caller must have forced that to happen, somehow.

Which meant that the caller was up to no good.

"What do you want?" Wahlman said.

"I want to know that I'm speaking to Rock Wahlman."

"Yes. This is Rock Wahlman. What do you want?"

"I'll be in touch," the caller said. "Make sure to leave the phone on. You wouldn't want to miss my call."

Click.

Wahlman slid the phone back into his pocket. Someone must have gotten to Kasey's parents. Probably not the private investigator working with Detective Collins down in New Orleans. A PI wouldn't have handled it this way. Probably someone working for the army colonel. The colonel using the codename *Dorland*. Probably an assassin. Which meant that Kasey's parents were in grave danger. And since Kasey was headed that way, it meant that she was in grave danger as well.

Wahlman needed to get to the bus station. Fast. He needed to get there before Kasey got on a bus and left town.

He jogged down to the next intersection and waited for the light to change, and then he crossed over and started walking backwards with his thumb out. The light cycled and the traffic on the main road started moving again, slowly at first, then faster, the cars and trucks and motorcycles eventually whizzing by at fifty and sixty miles per hour, some of the vehicles powered by grid-generated or solar-generated electricity, some of them by magnetic turbines, and an increasingly-smaller number by fossil fuels. Lone occupants, couples, entire families. Babies in car seats, teens eating French fries, nurses heading in for another twelve-hour nightshift.

The technology behind moving people from one place to another had changed at an alarming pace since, say, the middle of the nineteenth century. But when you got down to it, the people being moved hadn't changed much at all. They were basically the same as they'd been for hundreds of thousands of years. Cautious. Self-preserving. Fearful of the unknown. Wahlman was a big man, tall and muscular and bearded and scarred. And he was walking alone. Hitchhiking at dusk on a busy highway. A frightening sight in frightening times. None of the drivers even glanced his way. It was almost as if he was invisible. As if the act of turning their heads and acknowledging his existence would somehow put them in danger. He didn't want to call a cab. He didn't want to wait that long. The bus station was only three or four miles away. A five minute drive. Ten at the most, even with the current traffic conditions.

If someone would just pull over to the shoulder and offer him a ride.

And then someone did.

Someone driving a red pickup truck.

9

Kasey Stielson's parents owned a house in a subdivision on the outskirts of Nashville. Mr. Waverly had gotten their address and the code to disarm their alarm system from Colonel Dorland, and he'd driven there from the downtown tavern where he and Colonel Dorland had met. Nobody had been home when Mr. Waverly had arrived at the house, so he'd walked around to the back door and had picked the lock and had gone inside and waited.

And waited.

Why weren't they home? Colonel Dorland had said that they were retired. What do retired people do all day? Mr. Waverly had always thought that they stayed home most of the time, but maybe he was wrong about that. Maybe they were out playing tennis or bridge or taking a long walk in a park somewhere. Or maybe they'd gone on a trip. A cruise or something. It was possible that they weren't even in the country.

Mr. Waverly had been sitting at the kitchen table for several hours, and he'd been close to calling it a day when a car had finally pulled into the driveway. The deadbolt on the front door had clicked open and a man in his mid-to-late fifties had walked in and had headed straight down the hall to one of the bedrooms.

Mr. Waverly had followed the man, and had pointed a sound-suppressed semi-automatic pistol at his face, and had told him to get down on the floor and put his hands behind his back, and to be very quiet if he wanted to live.

Mr. Waverly had asked the man his name as he wrapped his wrists with duct tape.

"Dean," the man had said.

"Where's your wife, Dean?"

"She's out of town."

"So I don't have to worry about her walking into the house anytime soon?"

"No."

"I need to speak with your daughter, Dean. I need to speak with Kasey."

"She doesn't live here anymore."

"Where does she live?"

"I don't know."

"I find that hard to believe, Dean. I have a pair of pliers in my pocket. I don't want to use them, but I will if I have to."

"She's been traveling around the country with some guy. He's in some kind of trouble. She won't tell us where she is."

Dean's fingers were trembling, and his voice was quivering. He wasn't used to this kind of thing. He would crack easily. Like a raw egg. Which, of course, was exactly what Mr. Waverly had been depending on.

"I want you to give me her phone number," Mr. Waverly had said.

"She doesn't have a phone."

"Am I going to have to get the pliers out, Dean?"

"Please. I have money. You can have anything you want."

"I don't want your money. And I don't want to hurt your daughter. I have business with the man she's traveling with. I need to speak to him, and the only way I know how to do that is through her."

"What kind of business?"

"That's not your concern. All you have to do is give me the phone number."

"You're not going to hurt Kasey?"

"No."

"I don't remember the number," Dean said. "It's on my cell phone. On my list of contacts."

"And where's your cell phone?"

"Outside. In my car."

Mr. Waverly had walked out to Dean's car and had picked up the phone from the center console, and then he had moved the car into the garage and had walked back into the house and had called Kasey's number, using an expensive and illegal mobile application that automatically pinpointed the location of any cell phone in any part of the country.

As it happened, Kasey hadn't answered the call.

Rock Wahlman had answered the call.

Which was nice, because that was who Mr. Waverly had wanted to locate anyway. Now all he had to do was contact the nearest Sun River satellite office, which he was in the process of doing now.

In a few short hours, he would call Colonel Dorland and tell him the good news.

Everybody happy.

Except Rock Wahlman, of course.

10

Tan Jacket climbed out of the driver side.

He was holding a tire iron this time.

Red sweatshirt climbed out of the passenger side.

He was holding a baseball bat.

The two men started walking toward Wahlman. They stopped when they were about five feet from where he was standing.

"Need a ride?" Tan Jacket said.

"I do," Wahlman said.

"Unfortunately, my truck only has two seats. I guess you could climb in the back, as long as you don't mind the smell of the cow shit I was hauling earlier."

"I thought that was your breath," Wahlman said.

"You're a smartass, aren't you?"

"So I've been told."

"You hurt me a while ago. I almost puked."

"I'm going to hurt you again if you don't drop the weapon."

"What makes you think this is a weapon?" Tan Jacket

said. "Maybe I just stopped to tighten my lug nuts."

Red sweatshirt took a step forward.

"And maybe I'm heading over to the ball field for a little batting practice," he said.

"I need to get to the bus station," Wahlman said. "I'll give you a hundred dollars to take me there."

Tan Jacket didn't say anything.

Red Sweatshirt didn't say anything either.

They were thinking it over. A hundred dollars for ten minutes of their time. Fifty dollars each. It was a good deal. They should have taken it. But they didn't. Red Sweatshirt cocked the bat and took a swing at Wahlman's head. Wahlman ducked and barreled forward and rammed Red Sweatshirt in the gut, knocking him backward, into Tan Jacket, both of the men severely off balance now as Wahlman wrestled the bat away and drove the fat end of it into Tan Jacket's face, crushing his nose, flattening it out like a wad of bubblegum on the bottom of a shoe. Blood started gushing from Tan Jacket's nostrils and dripping from his chin. The tire iron clanged metallically to the pavement as he staggered sideways and collapsed onto a patch of scrub grass, coughing and retching and then lying there quietly with his hands cupped over the part of his face that used to be a nose.

Red Sweatshirt was still on his feet. He reached into his pocket, the same pocket Wahlman had seen him reach into twice before, only this time he actually produced the object he'd only thought about producing the other two times, a small semi-automatic handgun, probably a .22, a weapon that some knucklehead in some barroom in some part of the world might have referred to as a peashooter, but a weapon that was deadly nonetheless, especially at close range, especially if it had been loaded with hollow point rounds, which it probably had.

Wahlman was still holding the baseball bat.

"Put the gun away," he said.

Red Sweatshirt didn't say anything. And he didn't put the gun away. He aimed the barrel at Wahlman's chest. There was a bright flash and a loud crack as the bullet exited the pistol. But Red Sweatshirt's aim was off. Way off. Because at the very same instant he pulled the trigger, Wahlman unleashed a world class swing, the kind of swing that sends baseballs out of stadiums, the kind that gets you a standing ovation and an eight-figure contract and the girl of your dreams.

The pistol went flying into the darkness as the shattered fingers that had been holding it started to swell, as the intricate webs of severely damaged neurons expedited a series of throbbing wailing flashing messages that traveled up through the affected extremity to an area of the brain called the thalamus, an unequivocal memorandum stressing that this was going to be the worst pain that Red Sweatshirt would ever experience, that it would last a long, long time, and that it would never subside completely, no matter how many medications were administered, no matter how many surgeries were performed.

Having received and processed this urgent bulletin in less than a second, Red Sweatshirt started pacing around in circles, shouting and grunting and cradling his ruined hand close to his chest in a futile attempt to dial the agony down to a level that was merely unbearable. He turned toward Wahlman and said something incomprehensible, and then he staggered over to the grassy area where Tan Jacket was lying and collapsed there in the shadows beside him.

Wahlman walked past the two men and climbed into the truck. He pulled the cell phone out of his pocket to make sure there weren't any messages on it. There weren't. He released the emergency brake and slid the shifter into gear and eased onto the highway. It took him seven minutes to get to the bus station. Seven minutes of weaving through traffic and tailgating and flashing the headlights from low-beam to high-beam. Seven minutes of accelerating through traffic signals when they were yellow, and honking through them when they were red.

Seven minutes.

Not bad, considering the vehicle he was driving and the time of day it was. He parked the truck and ran inside and started looking around. He looked in the waiting area and the ticket lines and the gift shop, and he stood outside the ladies' restroom for a few minutes and he checked the snack bar. He walked out to where the buses were parked and looked inside every one of them.

Kasey was not there.

He'd missed her, and he didn't know where she was going. Not exactly. He knew she was going to a lake house that belonged to her parents, and he knew that it was somewhere in Tennessee. Somewhere around Nashville, but

Kasey had wanted to keep her daughter's precise location a secret, even from Wahlman.

Supposedly, the army didn't know about the lake house. Which meant that Colonel Dorland didn't know about it. Which meant that the man who'd called the cell phone didn't know about it.

Yet the man who'd called the cell phone had gotten to Kasey's parents somehow. He must have, because he'd gotten the number from somewhere, and Kasey's parents were the only people on the planet—other than Kasey herself, of course, and Rock Wahlman—who knew what the number was.

Dad's going to drive up to the house in Nashville to get an air mattress for me to sleep on.

Maybe that was it. Maybe the guy who'd called the cell phone had been waiting at the house in Nashville when Kasey's dad had arrived there. Wahlman didn't know Kasey's dad, but he knew that he loved Kasey, and he knew that he wouldn't have given up the number voluntarily, that he must have been coerced, threatened, maybe told that great harm would come to him and his family if he didn't cooperate.

Wahlman walked over to the waiting area and sat on one of the plastic chairs and pulled the cell phone out again. The ringer was on, with the volume turned all the way up, and the vibrate function was on as well, but he wanted to be absolutely certain that the man who'd called earlier hadn't tried to call again.

It appeared that he hadn't.

And then it occurred to Wahlman that maybe he never would.

Make sure to leave the phone on. You wouldn't want to miss my call.

Which made it sound as though further instructions would be coming at some point. A ransom demand, maybe. Not for cash, but for an exchange. The caller probably intended to use Kasey's dad as a bargaining chip, hoping to force Wahlman to be at a certain place at a certain time.

That was the implication.

But maybe that wasn't really the plan.

Maybe the caller wasn't really interested in forcing Wahlman to go anywhere.

Maybe the caller already had what he wanted.

Wahlman's location.

There was a reason Wahlman didn't ordinarily carry a cell phone. Too easy to hack, too easy to track. Even the burners, like the one Kasey had bought, if you had the number.

And the caller had the number.

Wahlman had been thinking about it earlier, about the caller being able to track his location, but he hadn't been worrying about it much, because he'd assumed that the caller was somewhere far away. If you're in Des Moines, for example, how useful is it going to be to know that the person you're looking for is in Houston? Especially if the person you're looking for is constantly on the move. By the time you get to Houston, the person you're looking for will be somewhere else. It's not likely that you'll ever catch up.

Unless you're more than one person.

Maybe Detective Collins and his private investigator had orchestrated this whole thing after all. Maybe local, state, and federal police agencies were involved. Maybe those agencies now had the number to the cell phone in Wahlman's hand.

If that was the case, he needed to ditch the phone immediately.

But what if that wasn't the case? What if the man who'd called earlier really was going to call back with some kind of ransom demand?

If Collins, or someone hired by Collins, had managed to get the number to the phone, Wahlman would probably be arrested soon. If Dorland, or someone hired by Dorland, had managed to get the number to the phone, further instructions would probably come soon.

Or a bullet.

It didn't seem likely that Dorland had tapped into some sort of independent coast-to-coast network of hired killers, but Wahlman supposed it was possible.

He stood and headed toward the exit. As he passed through the doorway that led to the parking area, he thought about dropping the phone into the trash can. But he didn't. He decided it would be best to hang onto it for now. If he suddenly found himself surrounded by police, then so be it. Maybe that would be the least perilous thing that could happen at this point. Wahlman would be taken into custody, but at least he would know that Kasey and her family weren't going to be dealing with some sort of abduction situation.

He walked out to the truck and opened the driver side door and slid in behind the wheel. Sat there and debated with himself over what to do next. If anything. You don't spend twenty years as a master-at-arms in the United States Navy without learning to be patient in a wide variety of situations. Wahlman wanted to head for Tennessee, but he was afraid that his current batch of trouble might follow him there. He was afraid that his presence might make things worse. Kasey didn't need that. And her parents didn't need that. And her daughter definitely didn't need that.

So maybe it was best to just check into a hotel and wait. Eventually the caller would call back, or the police would show up, or a hired killer would make a move.

Wahlman slid the key into the ignition and started the engine.

And then the cell phone trilled.

Wahlman answered.

It wasn't the man who'd called earlier.

And it wasn't Kasey, or either of her parents.

It was someone Wahlman had never talked to before. Someone he'd never expected to talk to—ever.

It was his mother.

11

While everyone else had left the office hours ago, Craig Pullimon was still sitting at his desk, working on the payroll for the week. He wanted to get it out of the way so he could take off early tomorrow and play some golf with his boss.

Work hard, play hard.

That was Craig Pullimon's philosophy, and he'd done well with it at Sun River Disposal, going from material handler to assistant office manager in a little less than three years. He drove a fairly nice car and he lived in a fairly nice house in a fairly nice suburb. He was still single and he did okay with the ladies, and he'd managed to save quite a bit of money toward his next big purchase—a set of jet skis and trailer to haul them with.

Craig had managed to save quite a bit, but he was still about a year away from making it happen. That was one of the reasons he wanted to hit the links with his boss tomorrow. He wanted to ask for a raise, to speed the process along a little. It's always easier to talk someone into something like that after a few holes of golf and a few cans of beer. And of course it didn't hurt that his boss was a fellow Marine Corps veteran.

Craig was transferring some funds from one Sun River checking account to another when the cell phone in his left front pocket started vibrating—the special encrypted device he'd been issued after a series of private meetings with a man named Waverly.

Which meant that a man named Waverly was calling now.

Which was a good thing, especially if you needed some extra cash for one reason or another. Mr. Waverly managed the office in Nashville, and he coordinated the secret afterhours assignments that he often referred to as *side jobs*. The last time Mr. Waverly had called, Craig had been able to put a nice down payment on the house he was living in now.

"Hello?" Craig said.

"Can you take a job for me?" Mr. Waverly said.

"How soon?"

"Tonight."

"You mean you want the initial assessment performed tonight, right?"

"No," Mr. Waverly said. "I mean I need for the entire job to be completed tonight. I can call someone else if you don't think you can handle it."

"I can handle it," Craig said. "No problem. Got a number for me?"

Mr. Waverly gave Craig the target's cell phone number, which would allow Craig to track the target's exact location in real time.

"His name's Rock Wahlman," Mr. Waverly said. "He's six feet four inches tall, and he weighs two hundred and thirty pounds. It's still pretty chilly there where you are, so he's probably wearing a jacket. Light brown, all-weather material, and maybe a navy watch cap. I'll email some photographs to you."

"Where is he right now?" Craig asked.

"At the bus station."

"He's leaving town?"

"Maybe. That's why I need you to hurry."

"I'm on it," Craig said.

Mr. Waverly disconnected.

Craig set the security alarm and turned all the lights off on his way out of the office. There was a suitcase in the trunk of his car that contained everything he would need for the job.

Easy money.

Now he would definitely be able to get those jet skis he'd been wanting.

12

Wahlman switched off the ignition.

"How do I know it's really you?" he asked the woman claiming to be his mother.

"I guess there's no way for me to prove it," the woman said. "It's not like we even share the same DNA or anything. I was just a surrogate. Actually, I guess *incubator* would be a more accurate term. They implanted the fetus after—"

"I know about all that," Wahlman said. "What's your name?"

"Joanne."

"How old are you?"

"Sixty-four."

"How did you get this number?"

"A man called me and told me you didn't have long to live. He gave me the number, said it was up to me if I wanted to contact you or not."

"Someone from the army?" Wahlman asked.

"He wouldn't identify himself. But it must have been someone from the army, now that you mention it. Who else would have even known about me?"

"And he said I didn't have long to live?"

"That's what he said. I was very sorry to hear that. Are you ill?"

"Why did you decide to call?" Wahlman asked, ignoring the question about his health.

"I don't know. It seemed like the right thing to do."

"Why now? Why did you wait until you thought I was dying?"

"Well, I never knew—"

"I was raised in an orphanage," Wahlman said. "You're nothing to me. An incubator, like you said. But I'm glad you called, because now I know what I need to do."

"Why are you being so rude to me?"

"I'm almost forty-one years old. I've gone this long without a mother, so—"

"You don't carry a baby for nine months and not form an attachment," Joanne said. "Even when it's not really your baby. I wanted to keep you, but the army wouldn't let me. I'd signed a bunch of papers before the—"

"They cancelled the experiment," Wahlman said. "You could have worked something out. Instead, I was given a fake history and sent to that shithole in Memphis for eighteen years."

"I'm sorry."

"The cells used for the cloning procedure were taken from a man named Jack Reacher. Do you know anything about him?"

"No. They didn't even tell me the donor's name."

"Don't ever try to call me again," Wahlman said.

He hung up.

Started the engine.

It was time to return the pickup truck to its rightful owner.

He steered out of the parking area and started backtracking, minding the speed limit this time and stopping at all the red lights. He made a U-turn, and then he pulled over to the side of the road. Tan Jacket and Red Sweatshirt were still lying in the scrub grass beyond the shoulder. Wahlman climbed out of the truck and walked over there and watched them for a few seconds. Neither of them was conscious, but they were both still breathing. Red Sweatshirt's right hand looked like a catcher's mitt. Tan Jacket was lying on his side. Wahlman couldn't see his face. And he didn't want to. He started to feel sorry for the men, and then he remembered that they had intended to kill him. He figured they still would if they got the chance. He didn't despise either one of them more than the other, so the decision to slide the cell phone into Tan Jacket's pocket was purely random.

Wahlman's original theory had been correct. Someone had gotten the number to the cell phone, probably from Kasey's dad when he went to Nashville to get the air mattress, and now someone was tracking the phone. Someone hired by Colonel Dorland. An assassin.

A man called me and told me you didn't have long to live.

A kind and thoughtful gesture, Wahlman thought. Allowing him to talk to his mother before drilling a bullet into his brain. Good old Colonel Dorland. What a sport.

Wahlman tossed the truck keys onto the strip of grass between Tan Jacket and Red Sweatshirt, and then he started walking toward the strip of hotels down by the interstate. He saw a marquis advertising a price he liked, walked into the lobby and paid cash for one night. He asked the clerk for a toothbrush and some toothpaste. She cheerfully handed the items across the desk to him, along with a key card and a paper receipt. The room was on the second floor. Wahlman took the elevator. He was tired of walking. Tired in general. He opened the door and slid the *DO NOT DISTURB* sign onto the handle and peeled his clothes off and took a shower. He used the room phone to call Message Moi and leave a voicemail for Kasey, and then he climbed into bed naked and switched on the television and fell asleep.

13

The sniper's rifle in Craig's suitcase was equipped with laser sights and a sound suppressor and a penetrating infrared scope—an illegal military-grade device that sold for more money on the black market than Craig made in a year, a device you could literally see through walls with. Craig assembled the rifle, and then he accessed the locator software on his tablet computer and tapped in the cell phone number Colonel Dorland had given him. A street map appeared on the screen, along with a flashing green dot that indicated the location of the phone.

Craig zoomed in on the dot. The phone was on the east side of town, near a major thoroughfare, several miles from the bus station. Which meant that Wahlman hadn't left town. Which was a good thing.

But the dot wasn't moving. Not even a little bit. Which didn't make sense, really, based on the location, unless Wahlman had thrown the phone away, or unless he'd decided to camp there on the side of the highway. Or unless he was already dead, which didn't seem likely.

Craig set the auditory alarm on his tablet to beep loudly if the phone moved, even an inch, and then he started his car and headed toward the east side.

When Mr. Waverly contacted you for a side job, it was understood that the target was to disappear without a trace, and it was understood that a DNA specimen would be preserved for confirmation. And, most importantly, it was understood that there would be no eyewitnesses and that nothing would be caught on camera.

Which made it crucial for you to take your shot from a distance.

A hundred yards was a good rule of thumb, but the further the better, really, as long as you were confident in a positive outcome. Once the target was down, you could assess the witness situation and advance to the area Mr. Waverly referred to as the *exit zone*, and then you could draw a vial of blood or snip a lock of hair and start the removal and disposal process.

The best exit zones were private and contained. Abandoned buildings were ideal, but that hardly ever happened. Personal residences were good, as long as the target was alone, or as long as you didn't mind taking out whoever else was there. Same with hotel rooms. An open campsite near a busy highway? Not so great. Too many people and too many cameras. So Craig was relieved when the tablet started beeping. He pulled to the side of the road and saw that the green dot was moving now, and that it was moving very quickly. It made a left turn and then it circled around and came to a stop.

Craig zoomed in until he could see the name of the nearest building. *University Medical Center, Level One Trauma Center.* The phone had been taken to the hospital. Which meant that Wahlman had been taken to the hospital.

Which was not good.

Hospitals were extremely poor exit zones. Too much security, too many people milling around. Doctors, nurses, technicians, clerks. Not to mention the patients and their families. Lining up a shot wouldn't be a problem. But getting Wahlman out of there afterward would.

Then again, maybe not.

Craig eased back onto the highway and headed that way. He knew the area well. He knew that the trauma center was in a building that was separate from the main hospital, and he knew that there was a public parking garage directly across the street. Patients were treated and stabilized in the trauma center, and then they were transported by ambulance to the central emergency room half a block over.

It was true that hospitals were poor exit zones.

But Craig had a plan.

This was going to work out. He could feel it.

14

Wahlman had expected the phone in his hotel room to wake him at some point during the night. But it didn't. It never rang. At 5:27 he opened his eyes and switched on the bedside lamp and called Message Moi to see if Kasey had received his voicemail. A robot voice told him that the account had been accessed at 3:12 a.m. and that one message had been acknowledged by one recipient. Which was a little worrisome, because he'd told Kasey to give him a call at the hotel when she got the message. He'd wanted to tell her about the call he'd received on the cell phone she'd given him. He wanted to tell her his theory regarding that, and he wanted to tell her to stay away from her parents' house in Nashville. He'd wanted to warn her, but she hadn't called. Of course it was possible that she hadn't wanted to wake him at 3:12 in the morning, and it was also possible that the phones at the cheap hotel weren't working properly.

He took another shower and put the clothes he'd been wearing yesterday back on and walked down to the lobby. He stepped up to the desk and asked the clerk if there had been any calls to his room last night. The clerk told him that there had not. He asked the clerk if there was somewhere nearby where he could get a cup of coffee.

"You can get one here," the clerk said. "There's a breakfast area right around the corner, just past the restrooms."

"Thanks," Wahlman said.

He found the breakfast area and poured himself a cup of coffee, and then he pulled a pre-sliced bagel apart and slid the halves into a toaster. He stood there and waited until the bagel was hot and golden brown and he put it on a paper plate with some cream cheese and sat down at a table. He didn't like it that Kasey had received his message but hadn't called him back. The more he thought about it, the more he didn't like it. He needed to get the SUV. He needed to head toward Nashville. Nobody could track him now that he'd gotten rid of the cell phone. He was off the grid again. Invisible. The way he needed to be to survive.

He finished his breakfast and walked back to the lobby. There was a television behind the desk, tuned to one of the local network affiliates. The morning news was on. An attractive young lady with a microphone was standing in front of a sign that said *UMC LEVEL ONE TRAUMA*. According to the attractive young lady, someone had stolen an ambulance last night. Two emergency medical technicians were missing, along with the patient they'd been assigned to transport. Before the incident had occurred, the patient had been treated for a broken nose and severe dehydration.

The attractive young lady instructed someone named Ned to cut to a picture of the missing patient, a driver's license photograph taken two years ago. Wahlman recognized the man. It was Tan Jacket. In trouble with the law before. Considered armed and dangerous. Suspected of stealing the ambulance. There was a hotline number you could call if you spotted him.

Wahlman was pretty sure nobody was going to spot him. Ever again.

He was pretty sure that Tan Jacket was dead now, along with the emergency medical technicians, who just happened to be in the way.

Wahlman had planted the cell phone in Tan Jacket's pocket, which meant that he was somewhat responsible for whatever had happened to him. And he was okay with that. He hadn't intended for anything to happen to anyone else, and he was very sorry if something did, but there was nothing he could do about it. All he could do was continue trying to get to the bottom of why all this was happening and try to put a stop to it before more innocent lives were lost.

The hotel staff must have changed shifts at six. There was a different clerk working the desk. Wahlman asked her if anyone had tried to call his room while he was out. She clicked some keys on her keyboard and swiped at her monitor screen with her finger.

"There haven't been any calls to your room since you checked in," she said.

"Okay. Thank you."

"Would you like to go ahead and book the room for another night?"

"No thanks. I'll be checking out in a little while."

Wahlman took the stairs up to his room, used the phone to see if Kasey had left a voicemail via Message Moi. She had not.

But someone else had.

15

Mr. Waverly was furious.

Craig Pullimon had called him at five o'clock in the morning.

"We have a problem," Craig had said.

Mr. Waverly didn't like being called at five o'clock in the morning, and he didn't like problems.

Especially severe, irreparable ones.

Craig had followed the cell phone to a hospital trauma center. He'd maintained surveillance from across the street in a parking garage until the man he thought was Wahlman was discharged from the trauma center and loaded into an ambulance to be taken to the main hospital. He'd used the special scope on his rifle to see inside the ambulance, and he'd squeezed the trigger three times. Once for the woman in the driver seat, once for the man in the passenger seat, and once for the patient. Then he had trotted across the street to the turnaround where the ambulance was parked. He'd climbed in and had scooted the woman over to the space between the seats and he'd taken her place behind the wheel and had driven the ambulance to the special disposal facility where targets—and sometimes their vehicles—were processed, and he'd promptly discovered the huge mistake he'd made. The patient was not Rock Wahlman. The patient was a man named Speers. A career criminal. A smalltime hustler who'd experienced a variety of courtrooms and lockups in a variety of jurisdictions.

"How could you have messed this up so badly?" Mr. Waverly had asked.

"He had bandages on his face. They must have been soaked in a saline solution, which interfered with the infrared scope's ability to—"

"What part of *six feet four inches tall and two hundred thirty pounds* did you not understand? This guy's a pipsqueak compared to Wahlman."

"Sorry. He was on a stretcher in the back of an ambulance. The image on the scope was a little fuzzy, probably from all the electronic equipment back there. EKG machines and defibrillators and such. It was hard to tell how big or small he was."

"Now we have three bodies and a vehicle the size of a bread truck to get rid of, and the target's still out there."

"I'll find him," Craig had said.

"No you won't," Mr. Waverly had said. "As of now, you're off the job."

"But—"

Mr. Waverly had clicked off then. He was as angry as he'd ever been in his life, and he didn't want to hear another word from Craig Pullimon. He would deal with him later.

Right now he had his hands full. He was still at the house in Nashville, where he'd intended to keep Kasey Stielson's father hostage until he received confirmation from Craig Pullimon that Rock Wahlman was dead.

Now he had three hostages.

Dean's wife, Betsy, had shown up at a little after midnight, and his daughter, Kasey, had shown up at a little after three. Now Dean and his wife and his daughter were all in the back bedroom, all restrained with duct tape and gagged with washcloths.

It had taken some time and effort to persuade Kasey to reveal how she and Wahlman were keeping in touch, but she'd finally given in.

As they all do, eventually.

Human beings can only tolerate so much.

Mr. Waverly had accessed Kasey's Message Moi account, and had left a detailed voicemail for Wahlman.

Now all he had to do was wait.

16

Wahlman played the message.

"Kasey Stielson is fine," a male voice said. "As are her parents. If you would like for that to continue to be the case, you will do exactly as I say."

The man wanted Wahlman to be at a certain Nashville address by one o'clock in the afternoon. If he was late, someone would die. Maybe Kasey. Maybe one of her parents. The choice would be made randomly. If Wahlman still wasn't there by two, someone else would die. And so forth.

Wahlman rushed downstairs, exited the hotel and headed toward the bookstore. He needed to get the SUV back, and he needed to get it back now.

And he was willing to do whatever it took to make that happen.

Myers was sitting behind the counter again. Reading and smoking and drinking coffee again. He was reading the same book. He was almost finished with it.

"Where's my car?" Wahlman said.

"Where's my two thousand dollars?" Myers said.

"I couldn't get it. Mrs. Cappulista said you can have the boat back."

"Did you talk to Johnny?"

"No."

"You need to talk to Johnny. I don't want the boat back. I want my money."

Wahlman reached over and grabbed Myers by the shirt and dragged him across the countertop. Ashes and coffee went everywhere. The mug that Myers had been drinking from hit the floor and shattered into a million pieces.

"Where's my car?" Wahlman said again.

"I'll give you the car back when—"

Wahlman shoved Myers into the stack of boxes he'd offered to unpack for him yesterday. The boxes toppled and Myers stumbled sideways and slid to the carpet, instinctively trying to break his fall by extending his hand on that side, landing with a pained expression as his wrist folded back much further than it should have. He sat up and stared at the joint and massaged it with his other hand.

"Where's my car?" Wahlman said for the third time.

"I'm calling the police," Myers said, reaching into his pocket and pulling out a cell phone.

Wahlman walked over to where Myers was sitting and kicked the phone out of his hand. It hit the ceiling with a crunch and landed on top of one of the bookshelves.

"The next thing you pull out of your pocket better be my keys," Wahlman said.

Myers started massaging his wrist again.

"I think it's broken," he said.

"Want me to break the other one for you?"

"You're not going to get away with this," Myers said.

"If I break the other one, you won't be able to feed yourself or bathe yourself or wipe your own ass for a few weeks. If you would like for that to happen, just keep not handing over my keys for the next five seconds."

Myers clenched his teeth. His wrist had started to swell.

"They're in the cabinet under the register," he said.

Wahlman walked behind the counter, opened the cabinet door and grabbed the set of keys he'd given to Myers yesterday. They felt greasy, as if someone had eaten some bacon or something before handling them.

"Where's it parked?" Wahlman said.

"I drove it to work today," Myers said. "It's in the alley around back."

Wahlman exited the store and walked around to the other side of the building and climbed into the SUV.

Four hours later, he passed a sign that said *NASHVILLE CITY LIMITS.*

He pulled to the shoulder and checked to make sure the pistol in the glove compartment had a fully-loaded magazine, and then he continued toward the address the man on the Message Moi voicemail had instructed him to go to.

17

Wahlman just happened to glance down at the digital clock on the dashboard as it changed from 12:44 to 12:45. Which meant that he had exactly fifteen minutes to get to where he needed to be.

Which, according to the onboard navigation system, was physically impossible.

Which meant that someone was going to die.

Maybe Kasey.

Maybe one of her parents.

Which was unacceptable.

Wahlman took the next exit and steered into the parking lot of the first convenience store he came to. He screeched to a stop in front of the payphone and climbed out and punched in the number for Message Moi.

He entered the password and the code to initiate a new voicemail.

"I'm almost there," he said. "But I need more time. Just a few minutes. Please don't harm the people you have there with you. I will be there shortly."

He hung up and climbed back into the SUV and got back onto the highway.

12:51.

He floored the accelerator and started weaving through traffic, ignoring the increasingly stern warnings from the navigation system to reduce speed. At 12:54 he exited the interstate and took a right at the fourth light and a left at the next intersection and he drove for a couple of miles on a road with a lot of curves and hills and finally came to the turnoff that led to the address he was looking for.

12:58.

It was a nice neighborhood. The houses were fine big structures, most of them brick or stone, most of them on extremely large lots. Three or four acres, Wahlman guessed. Four-car garages. Trees and hedges and flowers and mulch. Every blade of grass trimmed to an exact height, every picket fence gleaming in the early afternoon sun.

It appeared that Kasey's parents had plenty of money, but Wahlman doubted that it would do them any good at this point. The only thing that would do them—and Kasey—any good was for him to crash through the wrought iron gate at the end of the driveway and speed to the concrete fountain at the center of the turnaround and skid to a stop and grab the pistol and tumble out of the SUV and scramble up to the porch and bang on the door.

Which he did.

At exactly one o'clock.

He'd slid the pistol into the back of his waistband, thinking there might be a brief window of opportunity to use it at some point, but when the deadbolt clicked past the strike plate and the intricately-carved wooden door swung open, he immediately knew that wouldn't be the case. A man wearing a dark blue suit and a ball cap and sunglasses stood on the other side of the threshold. A black bandana covered his nose and mouth and chin, and he was aiming a sound-suppressed semi-automatic pistol directly at Wahlman's face.

"You're late," the man said.

"Right on time by my watch," Wahlman said.

"The barrel of this pistol I'm holding was pressed against your girlfriend's forehead when you knocked. Another five seconds and her brains would have been splattered all over the wall."

"I'm very glad that didn't happen."

"You're going to die today. You realize that, right?"

"Maybe we can work something out."

"Are you carrying a weapon?"

"No."

"I'm going to ask you to step inside and lie face down on the floor, and then I'm going to search you. If you're lying—"

"It's in the back of my waistband," Wahlman said.

"Lace your hands behind your head. Then turn around. Slowly."

Wahlman laced his hands behind his head, and then he turned around slowly. If he was going to have any chance of making it out of this alive, now was probably the best time to make a move. He could have grabbed the man's wrist while simultaneously planting the heel of his boot into the man's instep, and then he could have used his weight to back the man further into the foyer and he could have taken the man to the floor and he could have beaten the man to death with his bare fists.

But he didn't. Because it wasn't just his life on the line. Kasey and her parents were somewhere in the house. If Wahlman tried something and didn't succeed, the man would probably kill all of them.

Of course it was possible that he would kill all of them anyway, but Wahlman didn't think so. That was what the black bandana was all about. And the ball cap. And the sunglasses. The man was making sure Kasey and her parents didn't see his face. That way, he could let them go when this was all over. The man had been hired to kill Rock Wahlman. He didn't care about the others. He was just using them for leverage until he could do what he'd been hired to do.

The man reached under Wahlman's jacket and pulled the pistol out of his waistband.

"Give Colonel Dorland my regards," Wahlman said.

"Pardon me?"

"I know that's not his real name. It's a codename. I was a master-at-arms in the navy for twenty years. I worked closely with intelligence officers sometimes. I know how they operate, and I know—"

"Walk backwards into the foyer," the man said. "Close the door on your way in."

"Then what?" Wahlman said.

"Then I'm going to shoot you."

"Do you even know what this is all about?"

"Actually, I do," the man said. "Colonel Dorland told me everything."

"What did he tell you?"

The man ignored Wahlman's question.

"Walk backward into the foyer," he said. "Do it now, or I'll make you watch Kasey die."

Wahlman walked backward into the foyer, pulling the door closed as he stepped past the threshold. This was it. He was going to die now, and there was nothing he could do about it. He didn't say anything. Thirty or forty seconds ticked by. Maybe a minute. Then he felt the cold barrel of the pistol on the back of his head.

Then someone knocked on the door.

"Anyone home?" a female voice said.

"Answer the door," the man wearing the black bandana said. "Tell her to come inside."

"It's probably just one of the neighbors," Wahlman said. "She probably doesn't know anything about anything."

"But she's here now. I can't just let her go."

"Why not?"

"Because your car's ten years old and it's sideways in the driveway and there are skid marks leading up to it. She's going to wonder about that. Then she's going to start thinking that maybe something's wrong. Then she's going to—"

"All right," Wahlman said.

He figured the man wearing the black bandana would put the woman with the others until the job was done. She would be unnecessarily traumatized, but maybe she would get over it in time.

Wahlman took a few steps forward and twisted the knob and pulled the door open. A middle-aged woman with a big smile on her face and an armful of brochures asked him if he was happy with his current swimming pool service.

"I'm pretty sure I can save you some money," the woman said.

"Come on in," Wahlman said.

The woman came on in.

Wahlman closed the door.

"This is such a nice neighborhood," the woman said. "How long have you——"

The woman screamed and dropped the brochures when she saw the man wearing the black bandana. She went from bubbly and cheerful to frantic and frenzied in a heartbeat. She started losing it. Totally. Tears were flowing down her cheeks and she was waving her arms and shrieking at the top of her lungs.

And then there was silence.

The woman slumped to the floor.

One bullet hole in the center of her forehead and one in the center of her chest.

"Why did you do that?" Wahlman said.

"You didn't really think I was going to let anyone leave here alive, did you?"

"We had a deal. I kept my end of it. Why would you want to kill anyone else but me?"

"Because of the voicemail I left you," the man said. "It's a loose end, evidence that could be used against me. Kasey—or her parents, if they have the password—could access the account and foreword the message to the police. Then every law enforcement agency in the country would have my voiceprint on file. Sorry, but that's just not going to happen."

Wahlman hadn't thought about that. The man was right. It was a loose end. Voiceprints were every bit as incriminating as fingerprints. Wahlman had made a huge mistake. He should have known that the man wearing the black bandana wasn't going to let Kasey and her parents go. He should have made a move earlier, when he had the chance.

Now it was too late.

Wahlman turned and faced the man wearing the black bandana.

Looked him directly in the eyes.

The man gripped the pistol with both hands and aimed it at Wahlman's heart.

The man didn't say anything.

Wahlman didn't say anything.

And then something very strange happened to the man wearing the black bandana.

His head exploded.

18

A bright ray of sunshine beamed in through a hole the size of a quarter, a hole located several inches to the left of the front door. Wahlman had heard the bullet whistle past his right ear. Either the shooter had been aiming at Wahlman and had missed by a fraction of an inch, or the shooter had actually intended to kill the man wearing the black bandana. There was no way for Wahlman to know for sure which of those possibilities was correct, so he continued to treat the situation as active and extremely hostile. He hit the deck and crawled away from the door, toward the living room, through the blood and the skull fragments and the chunks of brain tissue, grabbing the pistol that the man wearing the black bandana had taken from him earlier and the pistol that the man wearing the black bandana had been planning to shoot him with. As he crawled through the living room, toward a hallway that probably led to the first floor bedrooms, he considered a third possibility, that the bullet had been a stray round from a hunter, or from someone shooting cans off of tree stumps or something. The neighborhood was surrounded by hills, and Wahlman had noticed several paths winding away from the curvy road he'd driven in on, several single-lane dirt trails that could have led to hunting camps. So it was possible that a stray round had killed the man wearing the black bandana, but not likely. The odds of something like that actually happening were probably about the same as the odds of strolling down the sidewalk and being struck by debris from outer space. It was one of those things that could happen, but didn't. At least not often enough to worry about.

Wahlman made it to the end of the living room, looked back and saw the slimy red trail he'd left on the oak floor. He figured the damage to the house would be the least of Kasey's parents' worries at this point, but still. He didn't like seeing something so pristine turned to something so ugly.

When he rounded the corner, he heard moans coming from the end of the hallway. He stood with a pistol in each hand and carefully edged his way toward the muffled and distressed sounds. He turned the knob and pushed the door open and saw Kasey lying on the floor and a man and a woman he supposed were her parents lying on the bed, all three of them bound and gagged and shouting *hurry up and get us out of here* with their eyes.

Wahlman pulled the washcloths out of their mouths and unwound the duct tape binding their wrists and ankles. Kasey's mom sat on the edge of the bed and started sobbing uncontrollably. Kasey's dad put his arm around her and held her tight.

Kasey stood and pressed herself against the front of

Wahlman's body and dug her fingertips into the muscles on his back.

"I thought he was going to kill us," she said.

"He was," Wahlman said.

"What happened?"

"I'm not sure. He's dead. That's all I know."

"But—"

"I'll explain later. Right now I need to make sure it's safe for us to go outside and drive away from here."

"What are you talking about? Why wouldn't it be safe?"

Wahlman handed Kasey the pistol that had been in the glove compartment, the one she was familiar with.

"Stay here in the bedroom," he said. "I'll be back in a few minutes."

19

Craig Pullimon picked up the single brass casing from the ground and slid it into his pocket. He disassembled the sniper's rifle, pushed the individual pieces into their cushioned cutouts, snapped the suitcase shut and loaded it into the trunk of his car. He climbed in and started the engine and headed for home.

As far as he was concerned, nobody else needed to die today. He didn't have anything against Rock Wahlman. He didn't even know why Wahlman had been targeted in the first place. He didn't know, and he didn't need to know. These side jobs were nothing more than business transactions to him, and since it had been made perfectly clear that his services on this particular job were no longer required, there was no reason for him to care if it was ever completed or not. He didn't do this shit for free.

Of course nobody was going to pay him in dollars and cents for the excellent work he'd done just a few minutes ago—perhaps the most challenging kill shot of his civilian career, because of the distance—but he would be well compensated for it nonetheless.

The way he saw it, every day would be payday from now on. Sunshine and roses and root beer floats. Because the way he saw it, getting to breathe another day, and another day after that, was the best paycheck anyone could ask for.

How could you have messed this up so badly?

Several years ago, Craig had heard about another job that had been messed up badly. Another case of mistaken identity, where someone other than the intended target had been eliminated.

The operative responsible for the mistake had disappeared a few days later.

Nobody knew for sure, but the general assumption was that Mr. Waverly had personally taken care of him. And the general assumption from that point forward was that if you made a similar mistake Mr. Waverly would personally take care of you too.

Which was why Craig had been forced to personally take care of Mr. Waverly.

Craig had used the same technology he'd used to track Wahlman, the same software he'd been using to track targets for a while now. He'd pinpointed the location of Mr. Waverly's cell phone in a matter of seconds. According to the computer, the phone was inside a private residence in an exclusive neighborhood on the outskirts of Nashville. Which probably meant that Mr. Waverly was inside a private residence in an exclusive neighborhood on the outskirts of Nashville. Craig had driven down there and had found a nice flat ridge overlooking the neighborhood where the house was located, and he'd used the penetrating infrared scope to peer into the foyer. There had been no doubt in his mind that the man wearing sunglasses and a ball cap and a black bandana was Mr. Waverly. There had been no doubt in his mind, because a slight adjustment to the scope had allowed him to zero in and see through the disguise, almost as if it wasn't even there. No fuzzy static from stray currents this time, no bandages soaked in saline. The man who'd been standing on the far side of the foyer with a pistol in his hand was definitely Mr. Waverly, and he was definitely dead now.

And Craig didn't feel the least bit sorry for killing him.

20

Wahlman's idea of a lake house was a one-room cabin or an A-frame with a loft.

Dean and Betsy's place was something else entirely.

It was more like some kind of resort. Five bedrooms, a dining table that seated twenty, a multi-level deck and a pool and a boat dock, a finished basement with a game room and a gym and a sauna, everything impeccably maintained, not a single neighbor in sight. It was the kind of place you might like to stay for a good long time.

Unless you were Rock Wahlman.

He was sitting on the far end of the dock, alone, drinking a beer and watching a bobber, occasionally reeling his line in and checking the bait, mostly just thinking about what he was going to do next, where he was going to go.

And wondering if Kasey was going to come with him.

Natalie had returned from her houseboat adventure. She'd been there at the lake house by herself most of the day yesterday, wondering where her grandparents were, wondering why they weren't answering their phones. She'd been sitting on the front porch listening to some music when Wahlman's SUV, Kasey's rental car, Dean's pickup and Betsy's hatchback pulled into the driveway. Of course she'd been very happy to see Kasey, and of course Kasey had been very happy to see her. Everyone got cleaned up and Dean grilled some steaks, and after a very pleasant dinner and some nice conversation, Kasey took Natalie upstairs and talked to her privately for about an hour. She probably talked to her about some of the things she'd talked to Dean and Betsy about earlier, although probably not in as much detail. For instance, she probably didn't tell her about the dead bodies in the foyer at the Nashville house and about tripping the security alarm on the way out so the police would think that a burglar had been surprised by a door-to-door salesperson. She probably didn't tell her any of that, but she probably did tell her that Grandma and Grandpa could never go back to that house again—no matter what—until she told them that it was okay.

Scary stuff for a fourteen-year-old, for sure—or for anyone, for that matter—but Natalie seemed to be taking it all in stride. Kasey was a good mom. Wahlman was certain that she'd assured Natalie that her safety was of utmost importance and had never been in question.

Wahlman sipped his beer and watched his bobber. He heard footsteps. He turned and saw Kasey walking toward him. She was carrying a small cooler. She sat beside him and pulled two beers out of the cooler and dangled her legs over the side of the dock and tested the water with her toes.

"Still way too cold to swim in," she said.

"That must be what all the fish think too," Wahlman said.

"You haven't caught anything?"

"Not even a nibble."

Kasey stood and put her hands on his shoulders and leaned over and bit down gently on his right earlobe.

"There," she said. "Now you've had a nibble."

"Best kind," Wahlman said.

Kasey sat back down.

"Mom and Dad said you can stay as long as you want," she said. "And they said we can sleep in the same room from now on if we want to."

Last night Wahlman had slept on a couch in a bedroom that had been converted into an office, and Kasey had slept on an air mattress in one of the bedrooms that hadn't been furnished yet.

Separate quarters, which seemed like the proper thing to do under the circumstances.

"What about Natalie?" Wahlman said.

"What about her?"

"You're not going to feel weird about sharing a bed with me while she's in the same house?"

"She's fourteen. She knows I've been traveling with you. She's not stupid."

"Have the two of you talked about that kind of stuff?"

"Yes. It was one of the things I discussed with her last night. So don't worry about it."

"Okay," Wahlman said. "I won't worry about it."

Kasey took a sip of beer.

"We could live here indefinitely," she said. "You could do the work you need to do from here."

"What am I supposed to do about money?"

"Mom and Dad have plenty. They want to help you get your life back."

"They said that?"

"Yes."

Wahlman gazed out at the hills in the distance.

"What's up there?" he said.

"I don't know. Just woods, I guess. Maybe some hunting camps or whatever. I can't imagine that anyone would want to live up there on a permanent basis."

Plumes of gray smoke rose from one of the ridges. From a campfire, Wahlman thought, or maybe a chimney. Southeast of where he was sitting. Five miles away, or maybe a little further.

"I should probably leave tomorrow," he said. "Or maybe day after tomorrow."

"Why?"

"This is a safe place for you and your family. I don't want that to change because of me."

"Nobody knows about this place," Kasey said. "Really. We can be comfortable here. We can live like normal people."

The bobber disappeared and the line went taut. Wahlman gave the rod a quick jerk to set the hook, and then he started reeling in the fish. It was a fighter. Maybe a largemouth bass. Maybe four or five pounds. It was going to be difficult to get it up on the dock without a net, and

Wahlman hadn't thought to bring one with him. He hadn't anticipated catching anything bigger than a bluegill or a sun perch. With a bass that size, the rod would break or the line would snap and the fish would swim away with the hook in its mouth and die. Which would be a shame. Wahlman figured he could make a nice contribution to the dinner table tonight with a fish that big, even if he didn't catch anything else all day.

"How deep is the water right here?" he said.

"I don't know," Kasey said. "This is my first time here too, remember?"

"Can you run up to the house and get me a net?"

"Okay."

Kasey stood and bolted toward the other end of the dock, toward the shore and the boardwalk and the steps that led up to the back of the house, toward the storage shed where Dean and Betsy kept their fishing gear.

Wahlman adjusted the drag on the reel and gave the fish some line, just enough to ease the tension a little, hoping the fish wouldn't be able to swim deep enough to get the line snagged on something at the bottom of the lake. He kept playing with the drag and reeling the fish in a little at a time until Kasey made it back with the net.

"You're going to see the fish soon," Wahlman said. "I want you to dip the net under it and lift it out of the water."

"There it is!" Kasey shouted.

It was indeed a largemouth bass. It was beautiful. Seven or eight pounds, Wahlman guessed, bigger than any freshwater fish he'd ever caught in his life. It broke through the surface of the water, jumping at least two feet in the air, thrashing and whipping and opening its mouth as wide as it would go, frantically attempting to free itself, attempting to get back to its ordinary existence, back to the business of just being a fish in a lake in Tennessee. Wahlman tightened the drag and reeled it in closer, the rod severely bowed and probably near its breaking point as Kasey reached out with the net and scooped the enormous fish out of the water and pulled it up onto the dock.

"I've never seen a bass this big," Wahlman said. "Not even down in Florida."

"It's gorgeous. Daddy probably knows someone who could mount it for you, if you want to do that. Or we could just eat it."

Wahlman crouched down and wrestled the hook out of its jaw, careful to do as little damage as possible to the surrounding tissue. The mouth was opening and closing and the gills were fanning out and the slick muscular body was flopping rhythmically against the wooden planks as Wahlman brushed back the spiny dorsal fin and gently lifted the fish from the dock and slid it back into the water. It swam away immediately and disappeared into the murky depths.

Kasey seemed baffled. Astonished.

"It was too beautiful to kill," Wahlman said.

"But you worked so hard to get it up here."

"It takes a long time for a bass to get that big. It should be allowed to die of old age."

Kasey moved in closer, wrapped her arms around

Wahlman's waist and rested her head against his chest.

"I never knew you were so sensitive about things like that," she said.

"Don't let it get around," Wahlman said.

They stood there and held each other for a long time and Wahlman thought about staying but he knew that he couldn't. He knew that his troubles would follow him eventually. And as much as he enjoyed having Kasey on the road with him, and as much as he needed her help, he knew that her place was here with her daughter.

Maybe he could leave for a while and do what he needed to do and then come back and start over.

Maybe.

If Kasey still wanted him.

At any rate, he could leave the lake house knowing that Kasey and Natalie and Betsy and Dean would be all right, safe and secure in this isolated wonderland somewhere between Mont Eagle and the middle of nowhere.

Thanks so much for reading KILL SHOT!

For occasional updates and special offers, please visit my website and sign up for my newsletter.

My Nicholas Colt thriller series includes nine full-length novels: COLT, LADY 52, POCKET-47, CROSSCUT, SNUFF TAG 9, KEY DEATH, BLOOD TATTOO, SYCAMORE BLUFF, and THE JACK REACHER FILES: FUGITIVE (Previously Published as ANNEX 1).

THE JACK REACHER FILES: VELOCITY takes the series in a new direction, and sets the stage for THE BLOOD NOTEBOOKS.

And now, for the first time, 4 NICHOLAS COLT NOVELS have been published together in a box set at a special low price.

All of my books are lendable, so feel free to share them with a friend at no additional cost.

All reviews are much appreciated!

Thanks again, and happy reading!

Jude

Made in the USA
Lexington, KY
15 April 2019